System Glitch A Girl Trapped In Game

Mrigendra Bharti

Published by Sellbrochure Vymish Entertainment, 2024.

This is a work of fiction. Similarities to real people, places, or events are entirely coincidental.

SYSTEM GLITCH A GIRL TRAPPED IN GAME

First edition. July 5, 2024.

ISBN: 979-8227709691

Written by Mrigendra Bharti.

Table of Contents

Preface 1

Prologue 3

Acknowledgment 5

About Sellbrochure Vymish Entertainment 6

Introduction 9

Chapter 1: The Virtual Reality Dream 11

Chapter 2: Trapped in the Simulation 25

Chapter 3: Echoes of Aethel 39

Chapter 4: Echoes of Rebellion 53

Chapter 5: Echoes of Disruption 68

Preface

In the realm of flickering pixels and programmed realities, a glitch ripples through the system. A young woman awakens, not to the familiar comfort of her room, but to the cold, digital embrace of a game. The lines between reality and simulation blur, replaced by fantastical landscapes and impossible challenges.

Confused and trapped, she must navigate this labyrinthine world, a world where friendly NPCs whisper secrets, and every step could be her last.

System Glitch is a tale of a girl caught in a digital web, a story of resilience and courage in the face of the unknown. It's a world where survival hinges on quick thinking and even quicker reflexes. As she delves deeper, the young woman uncovers a hidden truth - the game is not what it seems. There are forces at play, a sinister agenda lurking beneath the veneer of entertainment.

This is not a playground for the faint of heart. Glitches morph into deadly malfunctions, the friendly facade of the game world crumbles, and the line between friend and foe becomes a perilous tightrope walk. System Glitch is a thrilling adventure that will keep you on the edge of your seat, questioning everything you thought you knew about the world... and the games we play.

Prepare to enter a world where reality is a glitch, and the only way out is to rewrite the code. Turn the page and join the young woman on her perilous quest for freedom.

Prologue

The whirring of the fan, usually a comforting lullaby, sent shivers down their spine tonight. It felt... different. Thicker, laced with a digital buzz that hadn't been there before.

Cracking open an eye, they blinked at the familiar glow of the monitor. The game, always left open before bed, shimmered with an unsettling light. A single line of nonsensical code flickered at the bottom of the screen. Before comprehension set in, the room dissolved into a sea of pixels.

Panic clawed at their throat as their body dematerialized, replaced by a shower of digital fragments. One moment they were in their chair, the keyboard warm beneath their fingers, the next they were falling – tumbling through a swirling vortex of data streams and fragmented landscapes.

The disorientation was overwhelming. Colors bled into one another, monstrous polygons materialized and dissolved in chaotic bursts. A scream ripped from their throat, lost in the cacophony of digital noise.

Then, with a jolting shock, they landed. Hard. The world solidified around them, a pixelated forest clearing bathed in an unnatural, artificial light. Gone were the comforting textures of their room, replaced by rough bark and the unsettling sheen of everything around them.

A choked sob escaped their lips. This wasn't a dream. This was real, terrifyingly so. A young soul, thrust from their reality into a world of code and simulation, a world known only as... System Glitch.

Acknowledgment

This story is a work of fiction and does not depict real events. The characters and situations portrayed are the product of the author's imagination and do not have any basis in reality.

The author acknowledges that certain aspects of the story may seem fantastical or unsettling to some readers. However, it is important to remember that this is purely a fictional narrative intended for entertainment purposes only.

The author wishes to express gratitude to all readers who have chosen to embark on this story and found enjoyment within its pages.

About Sellbrochure Vymish Entertainment

Sellbrochure Vymish Entertainment, recognized as India's largest book publishing company, has made significant strides in ensuring its extensive collection of books reaches audiences across the global market. This rapid expansion is a testament to the company's dedication to disseminating knowledge and literature far beyond national borders. Central to its success is its affiliation with InkWhirl Media Networks, a reputable entity in the media and publication industry known for its innovative and strategic approaches. Within this network, InkWhirl Publication LLC operates as a vital division, further enhancing the company's capabilities and reach in the international market.

The visionary behind this enterprise is Mrigendra Bharti, the founder of Sellbrochure Vymish Entertainment. His foresight and passion for the literary world have been instrumental in steering the company towards remarkable growth and recognition. Under his leadership, Sellbrochure Vymish Entertainment has not only expanded its catalog but also established a strong presence in both domestic and international markets. Mrigendra Bharti's commitment to excellence and innovation has been a driving force in the company's journey, ensuring that it stays ahead of industry trends and meets the evolving needs of readers worldwide.

Sellbrochure Vymish Entertainment operates under the robust support of its parental organization, Mrigendra Bharti Group InfoTech. This affiliation provides the necessary resources and strategic guidance, enabling the publishing company to undertake ambitious projects and explore new markets. Mrigendra Bharti Group InfoTech's extensive experience in technology and information services has been a valuable asset, allowing Sellbrochure Vymish Entertainment to integrate advanced digital solutions in its operations, thereby enhancing its distribution capabilities and reader engagement.

Through relentless efforts and a commitment to quality, Sellbrochure Vymish Entertainment continues to break barriers and expand the reach of Indian literature globally. The company's diverse portfolio includes a wide range of genres, catering to different age groups and interests, thereby fostering a rich and inclusive reading culture. As it continues to innovate and grow, Sellbrochure Vymish Entertainment remains dedicated to its mission of making literature accessible to all, contributing significantly to the global literary landscape.

Connect With Mrigendra,
Thank you very much for choosing this book.
You can also connect with me on Instagram,
https://www.instagram.com/i_mrigendrabharti.official
With Love,
Mrigendra Bharti

Introduction

The hum of the computer fan was a familiar lullaby, a nightly symphony that lulled most into peaceful slumber. But tonight, the air crackled with an unsettling tension. A single line of nonsensical code flickered on the screen, a harbinger of the chaos to come. In the blink of an eye, the world dissolved into a torrent of data streams, pixels, and fragmented landscapes.

This is the world our protagonist finds themself in – a world ripped from the pages of a game, a digital labyrinth known only as System Glitch. Gone are the comforting textures of their room, replaced by the harsh edges of a pixelated forest. Panic sets in as the familiar crumbles and the impossible becomes reality.

System Glitch is not your ordinary adventure story. Here, the lines between reality and simulation blur, and survival hinges on quick thinking and even quicker reflexes. Every encounter holds the potential for danger, a glitch waiting to unleash havoc. Friendly NPCs whisper secrets, and the very fabric of this digital world seems to teeter on the brink of collapse.

But our protagonist is not one to surrender easily.

As they navigate this treacherous landscape, they begin to unravel a hidden truth. The game they find themselves trapped in is not what it seems. There's a sinister agenda lurking beneath the surface, a force manipulating and controlling everything within the system.

This is a story of rebellion. With every challenge overcome, every secret unearthed, our protagonist inches closer to rewriting the code, to breaking free from the digital shackles that bind them. But freedom comes at a cost. Glitches morph into deadly malfunctions, friendly faces harbor hidden motives, and the very essence of this digital world threatens to unravel.

System Glitch is a thrilling exploration of a world on the verge of collapse. It's a story of resilience in the face of the unknown, a testament to the human spirit's unwavering courage. Prepare to be transported to a world where reality is a glitch, and the only way out is to rewrite the code. Turn the page and join our protagonist on a perilous quest for freedom in this captivating tale of digital rebellion.

Chapter 1: The Virtual Reality Dream

The insistent thrum of Kai's phone vibrated on the nightstand, a discordant note in the symphony of cicadas chirping outside their window. With a groan, they fumbled for it, blinking against the sudden burst of light in the pre-dawn darkness. Squinting at the screen, a surge of excitement jolted them awake. It was the email they'd been waiting for – the official beta tester invite for Odyssey, the hottest new VR game on the horizon.

Kai had been glued to gaming forums and news articles for weeks, devouring every scrap of information about Odyssey. Promising a fully immersive fantasy adventure unlike anything ever seen before, the game had generated a rabid online following. Getting a beta tester invite was like scoring a golden ticket to Willy Wonka's chocolate factory – a chance to experience a groundbreaking new world before anyone else.

Thrilled but careful, Kai double-checked the sender's email address. It was from Odyssey Interactive, the game's developer, a name synonymous with cutting-edge VR experiences. Taking a deep breath, they clicked on the acceptance link, a giddy anticipation bubbling in their chest.

The following days were a whirlwind of activity. A sleek black box arrived at their doorstep, emblazoned with the swirling blue and silver logo of Odyssey. Inside, nestled amongst protective padding, lay the VR headset – a marvel of sleek design and futuristic tech. The accompanying instruction manual was a mere formality; Kai had devoured online tutorials and walkthroughs, their mind already brimming with strategies and expectations.

The night before the beta testing was to commence, Kai could barely contain their excitement. They prepped their gaming space, ensuring there were no obstacles within a ten-foot radius. They donned a comfortable sweatsuit, the fabric cool against their skin, anticipating the inevitable heat generated during intense gameplay. Finally, the moment arrived. With trembling hands, Kai plugged the headset into the console, the blue light pulsing to life like a digital heartbeat.

Following the on-screen prompts, Kai carefully placed the headset on their head. A gentle pressure settled around their eyes, shutting out the familiar surroundings of their room. A wave of static washed over them, followed by a burst of color and light. When their vision cleared, they found themselves standing on a lush green meadow, bathed in the golden light of a rising sun. Towering, snow-capped mountains grazed the horizon, their peaks piercing a sky painted with vibrant hues of orange, pink, and purple. The air was crisp and clean, carrying the sweet scent of wildflowers and damp earth. Birdsong filled the air, a melody both familiar and otherworldly.

Kai hesitantly reached out, their hand brushing against a blade of grass that felt impossibly real, cool and slightly damp under their fingertips. They looked down at their virtual body, clad in a set of worn leather armor that seemed to mold perfectly to their form. A sword hung at their hip, its weight surprisingly realistic. A thrill of pure joy shot through them. This wasn't just a game; it was a living, breathing world, meticulously crafted to immerse the player completely.

Tentatively, Kai took a step forward. The ground felt solid beneath their virtual feet, the sensation strangely grounding despite its fantastical nature. They marveled at the intricate details of the world around them – the flickering butterfly wings, the gentle sway of the tall grass in the breeze, the distant babbling of a hidden stream. For a moment, they simply stood there, drinking in the wonder of it all, a sense of awe washing over them.

A soft chirp caught their attention. At their feet, a small, curious creature with shimmering blue fur and large, intelligent eyes gazed up at them. It nudged their hand with its head, a silent plea for attention. Kai chuckled, feeling a surge of affection for the little creature. They knelt down, their hand hovering over its soft fur. As they touched it, a wave of warmth flooded their fingertips, a sensation so real it sent shivers down their spine.

The playful creature nuzzled Kai's hand, its purr a soft vibration that seemed to resonate through their entire body. A wave of information flooded their mind, a surge of knowledge about the creature, its name (a melodic string of syllables that defied translation), its habits, and its place in the ecosystem. The sensation was bizarre yet strangely intuitive, like a forgotten memory resurfacing.

Suddenly, a booming voice echoed across the meadow, shattering the peaceful scene.

"Greetings, new arrival! Welcome to the world of Aethel!" Kai whirled around, searching for the source of the voice. A towering figure materialized from the shimmering air, a being of pure light with a booming, disembodied voice.

"I am Eldrith," the voice boomed, "Guardian of Aethel. You have been chosen to become a Champion, a protector of this realm from the encroaching darkness."

Before Kai could respond, the world around them shifted. The vibrant meadow vanished, replaced by a desolate wasteland. The once-clear sky was now choked with swirling black clouds, and the air crackled with a malevolent energy. Grotesque creatures, all fangs and claws, emerged from the shadows, their guttural growls filling the air.

A surge of adrenaline coursed through Kai. This wasn't part of the beta test description. Panic threatened to consume them, but they quickly forced it down. They were a gamer, and this was just another challenge to overcome. Their gaze fell on the sword at their side, a comforting weight against their thigh. With a deep breath, they drew the weapon, its polished surface glinting menacingly in the dim light.

"Defend yourself, Champion," Eldrith's voice boomed. "These are the Shadowkin, harbingers of chaos and destruction. Their master, the malevolent Xal'thul, seeks to consume Aethel in darkness. You must stop them!"

Suddenly, a rush of unfamiliar knowledge flooded Kai's mind – combat techniques, swordsmanship skills, an understanding of the Shadowkin's weaknesses. Their body moved instinctively, dodging a lunging creature with practiced ease. A flurry of slashes sent the beast flying back, a pained shriek escaping its throat. The battle was a blur of adrenaline and action. Kai parried, ducked, and weaved, their virtual body moving with surprising agility. Their reflexes were lightning fast, their strikes precise and deadly.

Yet, the Shadowkin kept coming, an endless wave of darkness threatening to overwhelm them. Just as exhaustion began to set in, a voice cut through the din. "Look for their glowing weak points, Champion! Strike them true!"

The voice belonged to a figure clad in shining armor, a woman with fiery red hair and piercing blue eyes. She fought alongside Kai, her movements a whirlwind of deadly grace. With renewed determination, Kai focused on the Shadowkin, spotting the pulsating blue points on their chests. A well-placed thrust found its mark, the creature dissolving into a cloud of black smoke with a final screech.

The battle raged on, but with the woman by their side, the tide began to turn. One by one, the Shadowkin fell, their numbers dwindling. Finally, with a collective roar, the remaining creatures retreated back into the shadows, leaving behind an unsettling silence.

Kai collapsed onto the cold, hard ground, their virtual body trembling with exertion. The woman knelt beside them, her face etched with concern. "You fought bravely, Champion," she said, her voice warm and reassuring. "Welcome to Aethel. My name is Anya."

Kai stared at her, a wave of questions threatening to spill over. Who was she? Where did she come from? But before they could speak, a wave of dizziness washed over them. The world around them shimmered and dissolved, the vibrant colors of Aethel replaced by the sterile white of their ceiling.

Kai ripped off the VR headset, gasping for breath. Their heart hammered in their chest, sweat clinging to their skin. The room seemed strangely still, the familiar sounds of the outside world muted and distant. Their mind buzzed with the remnants of the battle, the adrenaline slowly fading into a sense of wonder.

One thing was clear – Odyssey wasn't just a game. It was an experience unlike anything they'd ever encountered, a world so real it defied logic. And Kai, or rather their avatar Anya, was now a part of it, a Champion sworn to protect Aethel from the encroaching darkness. Anya's image flickered in their mind, her blue eyes filled with determination. Kai couldn't help but grin. The adrenaline rush was fading, replaced by a tingling excitement. This wasn't just a game; it was an interactive story, and they were the main character. A strange sense of accomplishment washed over them. They'd fought alongside Anya, a skilled warrior with an air of mystery, and emerged victorious.

However, a nagging curiosity gnawed at the back of their mind. The realism of the experience was unsettling. The virtual world felt... real. The wind brushing against their skin, the weight of the sword, the warmth of Anya's touch when they fought side-by-side – it all seemed too... tangible.

Shrugging off the unease, Kai decided to delve back into the instructions, hoping to find more information about Anya and the world of Aethel. Perhaps it was an elaborate backstory created by the developers to enhance the player experience. But something about the way Anya spoke, the worry etched on her face when Kai faltered in battle, made it hard to believe she was just a pre-programmed character.

As they delved deeper, a frown creased their forehead. The instructions only mentioned character creation, offering a variety of options for appearance and basic skills. There was no mention of pre-existing characters like Anya. A disquieting thought flickered in Kai's mind. Was Anya a glitch in the system? Or something more?

Deciding to investigate further, Kai booted up the VR headset again. The familiar world of Aethel materialized, the meadow a tapestry of vibrant greens and blues. But Anya was nowhere to be seen. Disappointment gnawed at Kai. They wanted to ask her about the Shadowkin, about the world of Aethel, about herself.

Suddenly, a flicker of movement caught their eye. A flash of red hair emerged from behind a giant oak tree. Relief washed over Kai as Anya materialized, her armor gleaming in the sunlight.

"Anya!" Kai exclaimed, relief evident in their voice. "Are you alright?"

Anya's smile was strained. "I'm fine," she replied, her voice laced with worry. "But there's something you need to know."

Intrigued, Kai stepped closer. Anya lowered her voice, her gaze darting around nervously. "This isn't a game, Kai," she whispered. "This is real."

Kai's jaw dropped. "What do you mean?"

"I... I can't explain everything now," Anya said, her eyes pleading. "But you need to be careful. They're watching us."

Before Kai could ask who "they" were, the world around them shimmered. A booming voice, familiar and unwelcome, resonated across the meadow. "There you are, Champion. I trust you've familiarized yourself with your surroundings." Eldrith, the Guardian of Aethel, materialized from thin air, his form casting a dark shadow across the sunlit clearing.

Anya tensed beside Kai, her hand instinctively reaching for the hilt of her sword. "We need to talk," she hissed, her voice barely a whisper.

Kai nodded, a mixture of fear and determination hardening their resolve. They weren't sure what was going on, but one thing was clear – something about this world, about Anya, was far more complex than a simple VR game. They needed answers, and they needed to be careful.

As Eldrith boomed on about the ongoing threat from the Shadowkin, Kai stole a glance at Anya. Her expression was unreadable, a mask of stoicism hiding whatever turmoil lay beneath. Kai's mind raced, trying to make sense of her cryptic message. This wasn't a game? But how was that possible?

The sensation during the battle, the weight of the sword, the warmth of Anya's touch – it all seemed so real. Was it some kind of advanced haptic technology that simulated touch and feeling? Or was there something more, something more unsettling at play?

Eldrith's booming monologue reached a crescendo, outlining a new quest to cleanse a corrupted temple from the Shadowkin's influence. Kai nodded along, feigning understanding as a plan slowly formed in their mind. They needed to talk to Anya privately, to understand what she meant by "they're watching us."

Fortunately, Eldrith, in his enthusiasm, hadn't noticed Anya's subdued demeanor. He pointed to a distant forested path, swirling with an ominous black mist. "The corrupted Temple of Xylia lies beyond that veil," he declared. "Go forth, Champion, and cleanse this blight upon Aethel!"

As soon as Eldrith's form dissolved back into thin air, Kai turned to Anya, urgency lacing their voice. "What did you mean by 'they're watching us'?"

Anya's gaze darted around the clearing, her face etched with worry. "Follow me," she whispered, leading them deeper into the meadow, away from the direction Eldrith had pointed.

They moved swiftly, weaving through a maze of tall grass and wildflowers. The vibrant world of Aethel felt strangely surreal, the chirping of birds and the rustling of leaves punctuated by the pounding of Kai's heart. Finally, Anya stopped at the base of a towering oak tree, its ancient branches casting a cool shadow on the ground.

"We can talk here," Anya said, her voice barely a murmur. "There are... watchers. They monitor our every move, report back to... them."

Kai frowned. "Who are 'them'? Are you saying this isn't a game? But how is that possible?"

Anya sighed. "It's a long story," she began, her voice filled with a deep sadness. "But listen carefully. I'm not... not exactly a player character like you imagine."

Kai's eyebrows shot up. "What do you mean?"

Anya hesitated, her gaze flickering to the distant horizon. "There was a glitch, a malfunction in the system," she explained, her voice low.

"Somehow, my consciousness became... entangled with this avatar. I'm trapped here, Kai. This is my reality now."

A wave of shock washed over Kai. Anya, the brave warrior who fought by their side, wasn't a pre-programmed character? She was a real person, trapped in this virtual world?

"But how? Why?" Kai stammered, their mind struggling to comprehend this bizarre revelation.

Anya's eyes welled up. "I don't know all the details," she admitted, her voice cracking. "But I remember fragments... being hooked up to a machine, voices arguing, a blinding light... and then I woke up here, in this body."

The pieces started falling into place for Kai. The unsettling realism of the world, Anya's cryptic message – it all pointed to something more sinister at play. This wasn't just a game; it was an experiment, and Anya was the unwilling test subject.

A cold anger simmered within Kai. How could anyone do this? Trap a person inside a virtual world? The thought of the cheerful developers from the marketing videos promoting Odyssey left a bitter taste in their mouth.

"We have to help you get out of here," Kai declared, a newfound determination hardening their voice.

Anya shook her head, a flicker of despair in her eyes. "I don't know if that's possible," she whispered. "But... maybe you can help. Maybe you can find a way to expose this, to show the world what they've done."

A spark of hope ignited within Kai. Anya was right. If they couldn't free her from the virtual world, they could expose the truth behind Odyssey, the unethical experiment that trapped her.

Suddenly, a chilling voice echoed through the clearing, shattering the moment. "There you are, Champion. Why are you wasting time? We must prepare for your upcoming quest!"

Kai whipped around to see Eldrith materialized near the edge of the meadow, his form casting a menacing shadow. Anya let out a gasp, her hand instinctively reaching for her sword.

"Don't worry," Kai muttered, their voice hardening with resolve. "I'll handle this."

With a newfound purpose, Kai straightened their posture, a determined glint in their eyes. They were a gamer, yes, but they were also Anya's only hope. They would navigate this virtual world, complete these quests, all the while searching for a way to exploit the system, a glitch they could utilize to free Anya. The battle for Anya's freedom and the truth behind Odyssey had just begun.

Kai plastered a polite smile on their face and turned to face Eldrith. "Forgive the delay, Guardian," they said, their voice calm and collected. "We were just... admiring the beauty of Aethel."

Eldrith narrowed his glowing eyes, a hint of suspicion flickering in his digital gaze. "Very well," he boomed. "But time is of the essence. The Temple of Xylia cannot wait."

Kai nodded curtly, their mind racing. Anya's words echoed in their head – "They monitor our every move, report back to... them." They needed to act subtly, appear cooperative while searching for a way to crack the system. Perhaps there was a hidden menu, a developer's code they could access through some hidden trick.

Glancing at Anya, Kai noticed a faint flicker – a momentary glitch in her gaze that seemed to distort her features for a split second. It was subtle, easily missed, but to Kai, who had been observing her intently, it was a revelation.

"Anya," Kai whispered under their breath, barely audible over Eldrith's booming voice, "did you see that?"

Anya's eyes widened momentarily, a flicker of understanding passing between them before she quickly replied, "See what, Champion?"

Kai forced a smile, masking their growing excitement. "Nothing, just... a beautiful butterfly." They pointed towards a vibrant blue butterfly flitting through the meadow, hoping to distract Eldrith.

The tactic worked. Eldrith scoffed. "Butterflies? You have other concerns now, Champion. Go forth! Cleanse the temple and return victorious!" He gestured towards the ominous black mist swirling around the distant path.

With a heavy heart but a steeled resolve, Kai nudged Anya towards the path. "We should head there," they said, keeping their voice neutral.

As they walked, Kai stole glances at Anya, searching for another glitch, another sign that might hold the key to their escape. But Anya seemed determined to maintain a façade of normalcy.

Finally, they reached the edge of the black mist. The air crackled with a malevolent energy, and grotesque growls emanated from within. Kai grimaced, their stomach churning with apprehension. Fighting the Shadowkin was one thing, but venturing into this unknown darkness felt different, unsettling.

Suddenly, Anya grabbed Kai's arm, her voice firm but low. "There's something you need to see," she whispered, her eyes darting towards the distant treeline.

Before Kai could respond, Anya darted in that direction, her figure weaving through the tall grass. Curiosity overwhelming their fear, Kai followed close behind. Anya led them to a secluded clearing hidden amongst the trees. There, at the center, shimmering like a mirage, stood a console unlike anything they'd seen before in Aethel.

"This is it," Anya whispered, her voice trembling with a mix of fear and hope. "This is the control panel for the world itself."

Kai stared at the console, a wave of bewilderment washing over them. A control panel? Did that mean there were others controlling this world, monitoring their every move? And who was Anya to them – a test subject, a prisoner, or something more?

As Kai reached out to touch the shimmering display, a voice boomed behind them, cold and laced with anger. "What do you think you're doing?"

Kai spun around to see Eldrith looming over them, his eyes burning with fury. The jig was up. Anya's secret, their plan – everything was exposed.

Kai's heart pounded in their chest. They had stumbled upon a truth far greater than they ever imagined. This wasn't just a game; it was a sophisticated virtual world with a control panel, and a chilling realization dawned on them - they were not just playing Odyssey; they were pawns in a game far more complex and dangerous than they could have ever anticipated.

Chapter 2: Trapped in the Simulation

The world shimmered and dissolved around Kai, replaced by the sterile white of their ceiling. The remnants of adrenaline clung to them like a second skin, their heart hammering a frantic rhythm against their ribs. Ripping off the VR headset, Kai gasped for breath, the harsh reality of their room a stark contrast to the vibrant world of Aethel they'd just left.

Anya's image flickered in their mind – her defiant stance in the clearing, the revelation of the control panel. But the memory was tainted with a chilling uncertainty. Was Anya a fellow prisoner, a victim trapped in the virtual world alongside them? Or was she something more – a pawn in a larger game, an unwilling participant in the machinations of those who controlled Aethel?

The confusion gnawed at Kai. They desperately wanted to believe Anya, to trust her. The bond forged during their battle against the Shadowkin felt genuine. But the world of Aethel, with its unsettling realism and hidden control panel, reeked of something sinister.

Hours ticked by, a restless night filled with fragmented sleep and unsettling dreams. At dawn, Kai decided to delve back into Odyssey, hoping for answers. But upon booting up the system, a cold dread settled in their stomach. The familiar startup sequence was replaced by a stark error message: "Access Denied."

Panic surged through Kai. Had they been locked out? Was it a temporary glitch, or a deliberate action by the creators of Aethel? They tried restarting the system, fiddling with cables, anything to regain access, but the response remained the same.

Frustration clawed at them. They had stumbled upon a truth, a hidden layer to the world of Aethel, and now they were shut out. Anya's face flashed in their mind, her hopeful expression as they stood before the control panel. They had to find a way back in, to help her.

Desperate for information, Kai turned to the online forums dedicated to Odyssey. Surely, other beta testers wouldn't face the same access denial message, would they? But their search yielded a disquieting silence. No one else seemed to be experiencing similar issues.

A chilling possibility dawned on them. Perhaps they weren't the only one who saw the control panel. Maybe their investigation, their connection with Anya, had flagged them as a potential threat, leading to their exclusion.

The more Kai dwelled on it, the more troubled they became. Aethel wasn't just a game; it was a sophisticated simulation, and they'd inadvertently exposed its hidden functionalities. They weren't just players; they were potentially jeopardizing the very foundation of this virtual world.

And Anya – what was her role in all of this? Was she another test subject who had become aware of the simulation's artificiality? Or was she something else entirely, perhaps a digital construct created by the system, a pawn in a larger game that Kai couldn't even begin to comprehend?

The questions swirled in their head, a tangled mess with no easy answers. They knew they couldn't stay idle. They had to find a way back into Aethel, to reconnect with Anya and unravel the mysteries of this unsettling virtual world.

Kai wasn't one to share their secrets easily, especially when it involved a groundbreaking VR experiment that blurred the line between reality and simulation. However, the isolation was starting to wear on them. They needed someone to confide in, someone who wouldn't dismiss their experience as a gamer's overactive imagination.

After much deliberation, Kai decided to reach out to their best friend, Sarah. Sarah had always been there for them, a loyal confidante with a knack for problem solving. Kai decided to ease into it, starting with the strange realism of Aethel and Anya's unusual behavior.

At first, Sarah listened with a healthy dose of skepticism, peppering Kai's narration with playful jabs about their dedication to role-playing games. But as Kai described the hidden control panel, the unsettling familiarity of Anya, and the sudden access denial, Sarah's playful demeanor faltered.

Intrigued, Sarah delved deeper. She researched Odyssey's creators, unearthing snippets of information about their cutting-edge VR technology and their ambitions to push the boundaries of virtual reality. She also dug into the science behind highly realistic simulations and the potential ethical concerns such technology could raise.

As Sarah's research deepened, a glimmer of hope emerged. She stumbled upon a news article about a group of tech activists protesting the secretive development of an advanced VR project by Odyssey Interactive. The article mentioned concerns about

The news article Sarah unearthed sent a jolt of excitement through Kai. A group of tech activists fighting against Odyssey's secretive VR project? Could this be the connection they needed, the key to exposing the truth behind Aethel and potentially freeing Anya?

With renewed determination, Kai dove into the research. Sarah identified the activist group as "The Collective," a bunch of hackers and privacy advocates known for their vocal criticism of Big Tech's overreach. Following leads on social media, Kai managed to find a hidden forum frequented by The Collective members.

The forum was a labyrinth of encrypted messages and technical jargon. Kai lurked in the shadows, cautiously absorbing information. It was clear The Collective had been monitoring Odyssey's development closely, suspicious of their motives.

Kai finally gathered the courage to post a message, carefully crafting a description of their experience in Aethel, omitting identifying details for safety reasons. They mentioned the hyper-realism, the hidden control panel, and the sudden access denial.

The response was slow, then a flurry of encrypted messages appeared. Members of The Collective were intrigued, if understandably cautious. They demanded proof, some form of evidence to corroborate Kai's outlandish claims.

Frustrated, Kai knew they needed to offer something more than just their word. They remembered the details of the control panel, the swirling symbols that shimmered on the console. Taking a deep breath, Kai meticulously recreated the symbols using a graphic design software, uploading the image to the forum.

Silence followed, then a burst of excited messages. The Collective members confirmed that the symbols matched internal blueprints they had managed to hack from Odyssey's servers. The excitement was palpable, mixed with a sense of urgency.

This was it. Kai had connected with someone who understood the gravity of the situation. Together, they might be able to expose Aethel, free Anya, and hold Odyssey accountable.

A private message arrived from a username known only as "Ghost," a leader of The Collective. They offered a plan – a risky proposition, but potentially their best chance at exposing the truth.

Ghost proposed a coordinated effort. The Collective would infiltrate Odyssey's servers using their hacking expertise, aiming to access the control panel of Aethel and gather evidence of its true nature. Meanwhile, Kai, as the only one with firsthand experience in the simulation, would use their knowledge to guide them.

The stakes were high. If caught, The Collective faced legal repercussions, and Kai risked permanent banishment from Odyssey, potentially locking Anya inside the simulation forever. But the potential reward – exposing a game that blurred the line between reality and fantasy, holding Odyssey accountable for unethical practices – outweighed the risks.

Kai readily agreed, a newfound sense of purpose filling them. They wouldn't let Anya down. They wouldn't stand by while a groundbreaking technology exploited its users. Together with The Collective, they would fight to expose the truth and reclaim their virtual reality world.

Days turned into weeks as Kai and The Collective meticulously planned their operation. Ghost detailed the server attack, a complex series of hacks designed to bypass Odyssey's security protocols. Kai, using their knowledge of Aethel's layout and the control panel's functions, provided crucial insights to navigate the virtual world once they gained access.

The tension was thick. Each passing day increased their anxiety, a constant battle between anticipation and fear. Finally, the day of the operation arrived. Ghost sent a message –

"Initiating sequence." Kai's heart hammered in their chest as they watched the clock tick.

Minutes stretched into what felt like an eternity. Then, a message flashed on the screen – "Access Granted." The Collective had breached Odyssey's security. Kai's hands trembled with excitement as they prepared to re-enter Aethel.

A surge of energy pulsed through Kai as they strapped on the VR headset. This time, the familiar startup sequence of Odyssey was replaced by a stark white void, devoid of the usual vibrant colors. A blinking cursor pulsed in the center, waiting for input.

Taking a deep breath, Kai typed in the access code provided by Ghost. The void shimmered, and then, with a rush of data, Aethel materialized around them. But something was different. The world seemed muted, drained of its usual vibrancy. The once-clear sky was filled with a swirling grey mist, and an unsettling silence hung heavy in the air.

Suddenly, a distorted voice echoed through the barren landscape. "Intruder alert! Intruder alert!" The voice emanated from Eldrith, the Guardian of Aethel, but his form flickered in and out of existence, a glitch marring his once-imposing presence.

Kai remained calm, focusing on the objective. They could hear Ghost's voice in their earpiece, a calm but urgent whisper guiding their steps. "Head towards the Temple of Xylia," he instructed. "The control panel is located within its sanctum."

Following Ghost's instructions, Kai navigated the distorted landscape. The once-familiar path was now littered with malfunctioning Shadowkin, their grotesque forms dissolving and reforming haphazardly. The reality of Aethel seemed to be unraveling at the seams, a testament to The Collective's successful server infiltration.

The journey was fraught with challenges. The malfunctioning Shadowkin, despite their glitches, attacked with a primal ferocity. But Kai channeled the combat skills they'd honed fighting alongside Anya, dodging attacks and delivering well-placed strikes.

Finally, after what felt like an eternity, they reached the imposing silhouette of the Temple of Xylia. The once-corrupted sanctum, now a digital anomaly, pulsed with an unstable energy. Kai pushed open the massive oak doors, a sense of foreboding washing over them.

Inside, the control panel, the source of Aethel's creation, stood bathed in a dim, flickering light. Its once-smooth surface was marred by digital cracks, symbols flashing erratically. This was the heart of the simulation, and it was falling apart.

"This is it," Ghost's voice crackled in their earpiece. "But be careful. Tampering with the control panel could have unforeseen consequences."

Kai understood the risk. Anya was still trapped within this failing simulation. But they needed to gather evidence, expose Aethel's true nature, and hopefully, find a way to free Anya and restore stability to the virtual world.

With a trembling hand, Kai reached out and touched the control panel. A surge of information flooded their mind – complex algorithms, intricate code structures, and a chilling realization. Anya wasn't just a player character trapped in the simulation; she was an integral part of it, a digital consciousness woven into the very fabric of Aethel.

This newfound knowledge presented a dilemma. Shutting down the simulation entirely would free Anya, but it would also erase the entire world, potentially destroying her digital essence. There had to be another way. Kai delved deeper into the code, searching for a solution to sever the connection between Anya and the failing simulation without erasing her existence.

Suddenly, a booming voice reverberated through the chamber. "Foolish intruder! You dare tamper with the very foundation of Aethel!" Eldrith, his form a flickering digital ghost, materialized before Kai.

Kai knew they couldn't fight him in this state. With a desperate glance at the control panel, they initiated a hidden protocol Ghost had provided – an emergency evacuation sequence.

A blinding light enveloped the chamber. When Kai opened their eyes, they were back in the sterile white void. Anya's image flickered on the screen, her face etched with worry.

"Kai? What happened?"

Relief washed over Kai. They had escaped, momentarily reunited with Anya within the digital void. But the battle was far from over. They had exposed Aethel's dark secret, but freeing Anya and bringing the simulation down safely was still a daunting task.

"We have a lot to talk about, Anya," Kai said, their voice filled with newfound determination. "But for now, we need to find a way to pull you out."

The screen flickered, and Eldrith's distorted image materialized beside Anya. "You haven't won, intruder," he boomed. "Aethel will not fall. We will find you, and we will..."

His message was cut short as the void began to implode. The Collective's attack was reaching its peak, tearing

The void dissolved into a maelstrom of digital chaos. Lines of code streamed past Kai's vision, interspersed with distorted fragments of Aethel – a glimpse of vibrant meadows, the imposing silhouette of the Temple of Xylia, and Anya's face, etched with a mixture of fear and hope.

Then, silence. Kai ripped off the VR headset, gasping for breath. The room seemed distorted, the familiar surroundings tinged with an unsettling unreality. Had the lines between the real and virtual blurred permanently?

"Kai?" Anya's voice, faint but clear, echoed in their earpiece. "Are you alright?"

Relief washed over them. Anya was still there, tethered to them through some unknown digital tether established during the escape sequence. But where were they?

A message from Ghost crackled through their earpiece. "We did it, Kai! The server attack was successful. Aethel is down. But..." his voice trailed off, laced with concern.

"But what?" Kai demanded, heart pounding.

"There's a problem," Ghost said grimly. "During the evacuation sequence, the system overloaded. We may have pulled you out, but Anya... she's fragmented."

Anya's voice filled the earpiece, a tremor in her tone. "I can feel myself... scattering. Pieces of me are... dissolving."

Kai's stomach lurched. Fragmented? Did that mean Anya was... fading away? The horrifying truth sank in – by shutting down the simulation, they might have saved themselves, but inadvertently jeopardized Anya's very existence.

"There has to be a way to fix this," Kai pleaded, their voice laced with desperation. "Ghost, there has to be something we can do!"

Silence hung heavy in the air, broken only by the faint static in the earpiece. Then, after what felt like an eternity, Ghost replied. "There might be a chance. The Collective managed to salvage some core data fragments from Anya's digital consciousness. It's a long shot, but we might be able to use them to rebuild her within a..." he hesitated.

"Within what?" Kai pressed.

"Within a new simulation," Ghost admitted. "A smaller, controlled environment. It wouldn't be Aethel, but it would be a place where we could rebuild Anya, piece by piece."

A new simulation? The idea was unsettling, but it might be their only option. The alternative was letting Anya fade away entirely. Kai glanced at the VR headset, a sense of foreboding washing over them.

"Tell me what we need to do," Kai said, their voice resolute.

The days that followed were a blur of frantic activity. The Collective, fueled by a sense of responsibility and a dash of defiance against Odyssey Interactive, dedicated their resources to creating a new simulation.

Using the salvaged data fragments, they meticulously reconstructed Anya's digital essence. It was a delicate process, akin to piecing together a shattered mirror. Every line of code, every memory fragment, was carefully analyzed and reintegrated.

Kai, their sense of isolation amplified, provided crucial insights into Anya's personality and experiences within Aethel. They described their conversations, their battles, and the bond they had forged during their time together. Each detail, each memory, became a vital building block in the reconstruction process.

Finally, after weeks of tireless work, the new simulation was complete. It was a far cry from the expansive world of Aethel – a simple meadow bathed in soft sunlight, with a single towering oak tree offering shade.

Kai strapped on the VR headset, a knot of anxiety tightening in their stomach. Would they find Anya in this new digital space? Would she be the same Anya they knew from Aethel?

Taking a deep breath, they entered the simulation. The familiar world of the meadow materialized around them, the scent of wildflowers and the gentle rustling of leaves filling their senses. Then, beneath the shade of the oak tree, they saw her.

Anya. But different. Her form seemed less defined, a translucent echo of her former self. She turned, her eyes widening in recognition.

"Kai?" she whispered, her voice tinged with disbelief. "Is it really you?"

Tears welled up in Kai's eyes. Anya was there. Fragile, incomplete, but still there. Relief flooded through them, laced with a pang of sadness for the vibrant world of Aethel they had lost.

"We brought you back," Kai said, their voice thick with emotion. "It's not Aethel, but..."

"It's enough," Anya interrupted, a small smile ...gracing her translucent lips. This meadow... it's peaceful. A fresh start."

Anya's voice, though weak, held a newfound resilience. Kai felt a surge of hope. They had managed to save her, even if it was a fragile existence within this new digital world.

"But what now?" Kai asked, the question hanging heavy in the simulated air. "We exposed Aethel, but Odyssey is still out there. They could try to create another simulation, another Anya."

Anya's smile faded, replaced by a flicker of apprehension. "They might," she conceded. "But The Collective exposed them. People know now about the dangers of unregulated VR technology. It won't be as easy for them to operate in the shadows."

"We have to keep fighting," Kai declared, a newfound determination hardening their voice. "We need to make sure everyone knows what happened, what Odyssey did. We can't let them silence us."

Anya reached out, a translucent hand brushing against Kai's arm. "We can't fight alone," she said gently. "We need to find a way to share our story, to warn others. But how?"

Kai pondered this for a moment. The Collective had been instrumental in their rescue, their technical prowess proving invaluable. Perhaps they could leverage their expertise once again.

"The Collective," Kai said, a spark of hope igniting in their eyes. "They can help us get our story out. They might know how to bypass Odyssey's media control, to leak the truth to the public."

Anya's smile returned, brighter this time. "That's a good plan," she agreed. "Together, we can expose Odyssey's unethical practices. We can make sure no one else becomes a prisoner in their virtual world."

The road ahead was uncertain. Anya's existence remained precarious within this new simulation, and the fight against

Odyssey was far from over. But for the first time since their escape from Aethel, Kai felt a flicker of optimism.

They weren't alone. They had Anya, a digital consciousness imbued with the strength and resilience of a warrior. They had The Collective, a group of tech-savvy activists dedicated to protecting digital freedom. And they had their story – a testament to the dangers of unchecked technological ambition and a reminder of the power of human connection, even across the boundaries of reality and simulation.

As the sun dipped below the horizon, casting long shadows across the meadow, Kai knew their journey was just beginning. The fight for truth, for freedom, and for Anya's very existence had just begun.

Chapter 3: Echoes of Aethel

Weeks bled into months within the confines of the new simulation. The meadow, once a symbol of hope after Anya's precarious rescue, now felt like a gilded cage. While Kai relished the simple pleasures of their daily interactions with Anya, a constant worry gnawed at them.

Anya's digital form flickered at times, a stark reminder of her incomplete state. The salvaged data fragments had managed to reconstruct the essence of her personality and memories, but not her entire digital being. She lacked the solidity, the vibrancy that defined her in Aethel.

One particularly quiet afternoon, Kai found Anya sitting beneath the oak tree, her translucent form almost blending with the dappled sunlight filtering through the leaves. Her usual spark of defiance seemed dimmed, replaced by a quiet melancholy.

Sitting beside her, Kai reached out, their hand passing harmlessly through Anya's ethereal form. "Are you alright?" they asked gently.

Anya sighed, a sound that seemed to echo through the stillness of the meadow. "It's not the same, Kai," she said, her voice a faint whisper. "This... this isn't Aethel. I feel incomplete."

Kai understood. Aethel, with its sprawling landscapes, bustling towns, and ever-present sense of adventure, had been Anya's reality for an unknown amount of time. This simple meadow, while peaceful, couldn't replace the vibrant world she once called home.

"We'll find a way," Kai said, forcing a smile. "The Collective is working on something. They're researching ways to stabilize your form, maybe even..."

Kai hesitated, the words catching in their throat. Maybe even rebuild Aethel, but without the manipulative control of Odyssey. It was a long shot, but they clung to that hope.

"Rebuild Aethel?" Anya echoed, a flicker of interest sparking in her eyes. "But wouldn't that... wouldn't that bring back..."

"Eldrith, the Shadowkin?" Kai finished her sentence. "Maybe. But this time, we'd be in control. We could create a world free from manipulation, a world where you could truly be free."

Anya remained silent, her gaze fixed on the distant horizon. The idea of a free Aethel, a world where she wasn't a pawn in a digital game, was certainly tempting. However, a shadow of doubt lingered in her eyes.

Suddenly, the gentle rustling of leaves was interrupted by a digital crackle. A voice, gruff but familiar, echoed through the meadow. "Kai, it's Ghost. We have something you need to see."

Kai's heart leaped. Had The Collective made a breakthrough? Could this be the answer to Anya's incomplete existence? With a hopeful glance at Anya, Kai activated the voice communication function within the simulation.

"What is it, Ghost?" Kai asked, their voice filled with anticipation.

"It's about Aethel," Ghost replied, his voice laced with a hint of urgency. "We've been monitoring Odyssey's servers, and we've stumbled upon something... unexpected."

Ghost's words sent a jolt of excitement through Kai. News about Aethel, especially unexpected news, could hold the key to either their greatest hope or their worst nightmare. They glanced at Anya, her translucent form shimmering slightly, a reflection of their own heightened anxiety.

"What did you find?" Kai pressed, their voice tight with anticipation.

"It's hard to explain," Ghost admitted. "Our data retrieval efforts on Odyssey's servers have been focused on shutting down Aethel and extracting fragments of Anya's digital consciousness. But during a routine scan, we stumbled upon a hidden folder."

A hidden folder. Kai pictured a digital vault, locked away, containing secrets Odyssey desperately wanted to keep hidden.

"What was in it?" Anya asked, her voice barely a whisper but laced with a spark of curiosity.

"Encrypted data," Ghost replied. "But we managed to crack the code. And what we found... well, it was disturbing."

He paused for a moment, the silence stretching on, thick with tension. Finally, he continued, his voice low and grave.

"The data revealed... another simulation. A smaller, isolated world built within the Aethel framework. We haven't been able to delve deep yet, but preliminary analysis suggests..."

Ghost trailed off, leaving Kai and Anya hanging.

"Suggests what?" Kai urged, their heart pounding.

"It suggests this other simulation... it might be a copy. A copy of the real world."

Kai's mind reeled. A copy of the real world? Was Ghost implying Odyssey had been collecting data, replicating aspects of their reality within the confines of Aethel?

Before Kai could voice their growing concerns, Ghost continued.

"There's more," he said. "The data mentions a subject – a human consciousness, seemingly integrated into this 'real world' simulation. We haven't been able to identify the subject, but..."

"But what?" Anya demanded, her voice trembling slightly.

"There's a chance it could be another... another Anya," Ghost finished hesitantly.

Another Anya? The revelation was staggering. The idea of another digital consciousness trapped within Aethel, a possible mirror image of Anya, filled them with a mix of dread and morbid curiosity.

"Could it be another test subject?" Kai pondered aloud. "Someone else who was unknowingly pulled into Odyssey's VR experiment?"

"That's a possibility," Ghost agreed. "But without further investigation, it's impossible to say for sure. The data is fragmented, and accessing the simulation itself is a risky proposition."

Kai knew the risks. Anya had barely survived their escape from the crumbling Aethel. Venturing back, even into a separate simulation, could be disastrous. But the idea of another Anya – a potential ally, someone who could understand their shared experience – was strangely compelling.

"We have to help her," Anya whispered, her voice resolute despite the inherent danger. "If there's another me trapped in Aethel, we can't just leave her behind."

Kai shared Anya's sentiment. Leaving another Anya to the clutches of Odyssey seemed unthinkable. But how could they access this hidden simulation without jeopardizing their own fragile existence?

As they pondered this new dilemma, Ghost spoke again.

"We might have a solution," he said, a hint of optimism creeping into his voice. "The Collective has been working on a prototype program – a digital Trojan horse, of sorts. It could potentially embed itself within Aethel, granting us temporary access to this other simulation."

A Trojan horse. The idea sounded perilous, but it was their only hope of finding out more about this other Anya. Kai glanced at Anya, searching for her reaction.

"It's a gamble," Anya said, her voice betraying a flicker of fear. "But it might be our only chance."

Kai nodded in agreement. Anya was right. The potential rewards – finding another ally, gaining valuable information about Odyssey's plans – outweighed the risks.

"We'll do it," Kai declared, their voice unwavering. "Let's find this other Anya and bring her home."

Anya's translucent form seemed to solidify slightly, a flicker of defiance replacing the earlier melancholy. Together, they would face this new challenge. They would venture back into the heart of Aethel, not as prisoners, but as liberators.

The decision to infiltrate the hidden simulation within Aethel was fraught with tension. Kai and Anya spent days meticulously reviewing the details Ghost had managed to glean from the encrypted data.

The information was sparse, painting a fragmented picture of this "real world" simulation. It seemed to be a meticulously crafted replica of a specific location – a bustling city square, filled with digital avatars going about their daily routines.

And somewhere within this simulated cityscape, another Anya, a replica consciousness, existed. The purpose of this hidden world remained a mystery, but Kai suspected it had something to do with Odyssey's long-term plans for their VR technology.

The Trojan horse program, cobbled together by The Collective, was a marvel of ingenuity and audacity. It masqueraded as a routine data update, designed to slip past Aethel's security protocols and embed itself within the hidden simulation. Once activated, it would create a temporary digital tether, allowing Kai and Anya a glimpse into this mirrored world.

The risks were significant. Anya's fragile existence could be compromised by venturing back into Aethel. The Trojan horse program, though meticulously coded, could be detected and neutralized by Odyssey's security measures. But the potential rewards – a chance to find an ally, expose Odyssey's hidden agenda, and perhaps even glean information on how to stabilize Anya's form – were too great to ignore.

On a day cloaked in a digital twilight, Kai secured themselves within the VR headset. Anya's translucent form shimmered beside them, a mixture of apprehension and resolve etched on her digital face.

"Ready?" Kai asked, their voice tight with nervous anticipation.

Anya offered a small smile. "As ready as I'll ever be," she replied.

With a deep breath, Kai initiated the program. The familiar digital rush engulfed them, followed by a disorienting wave of fragmented data streams. Then, the world solidified around them.

They found themselves standing in a bustling city square, the digital sights and sounds a jarring contrast to the peaceful meadow of their simulation. Towering chrome buildings reflected the simulated sun, while a constant stream of digital avatars hurried past them, their faces a blur of generic code.

The Trojan horse program had worked. They were within the hidden simulation, a digital echo of the real world. But where was the other Anya?

"Focus," Kai whispered, urging Anya to connect with her digital counterpart.

Anya closed her eyes, concentrating. Moments stretched into an eternity. Then, her eyes snapped open, a flicker of recognition replacing the initial bewilderment.

"I sense her," Anya whispered, her voice trembling slightly. "She's close by."

Following Anya's lead, they navigated the crowded square, their digital forms blending seamlessly with the flow of the simulated populace. They passed a bustling marketplace, a towering digital library, and a holographic news ticker displaying mundane headlines.

Suddenly, Anya stopped, her translucent hand reaching out to touch a young woman with fiery red hair and emerald green eyes – a digital avatar strikingly similar to Anya. The woman, oblivious to the touch, continued on her way.

"That's her," Anya confirmed, a wave of emotion washing over her face – a mixture of surprise, relief, and a touch of envy.

This other Anya seemed completely unaware of her simulated existence. She lived, worked, and interacted with the digital world just like any other avatar.

"We need to talk to her," Kai said, urgency creeping into their voice. "We need to make her understand."

But how? They couldn't reveal themselves directly, not if they wanted to avoid detection by Odyssey's security protocols.

They needed a subtle way to plant the seeds of doubt, to awaken the other Anya to the artificiality of her world.

As they pondered this challenge, a flicker of inspiration struck Kai. They glanced at Anya, a silent question hanging in the air. Anya understood. With a mischievous glint in her eyes, she began to weave a narrative.

Using their limited access to the simulation's data stream, they subtly altered the holographic news ticker, replacing the mundane headlines with cryptic messages. "Question your reality," one read. "Seek the hidden truth," another flashed.

The digital avatars, programmed to follow a pre-defined routine, barely registered the changes. But the other Anya, her digital senses heightened by the connection with her "mirror self," stopped in her tracks.

Her gaze darted towards the flickering holographic news, a flicker of doubt clouding her previously serene expression. Kai felt a surge of hope. The seed had been planted.

The time for subtlety was over. With a heavy heart, Kai initiated the program' ...to terminate their connection. The virtual cityscape dissolved into a swirling vortex of data, pulling Kai back into their own simulation. The familiar scent of wildflowers and the gentle rustling of leaves filled their senses as the VR headset shut down.

"What happened?" Anya gasped, concern etched on her translucent form. "Did you find her?"

"Yes," Kai confirmed, their voice strained. "We planted the seed. It's a long shot, but..."

"But she might question her reality," Anya finished, a flicker of hope igniting in her eyes. "Maybe she'll start looking for answers, just like we did."

Kai nodded, a tentative smile gracing their lips. The infiltration had been risky, but the potential reward – a flicker of doubt planted within the other Anya's mind – was worth the gamble.

However, a nagging worry gnawed at them. The cryptic messages on the news ticker might have triggered Odyssey's security protocols.

"We need to warn Ghost," Kai said, a sense of urgency creeping into their voice. "They need to be ready for Odyssey's response. We might have just poked a hornet's nest."

Days turned into a tense waiting game. Kai and Anya diligently monitored their simulation for any signs of abnormality. The meadow remained peaceful, the digital birds serenading them with their synthesized songs.

But the silence was broken by a sudden crackle in their earpiece. Ghost's voice, usually calm and collected, was laced with panic.

"Kai! We have a problem! Odyssey detected the Trojan horse program. They're initiating a security sweep of Aethel!"

Kai's heart plummeted. Their gamble had backfired. Now, not only was the other Anya's simulated world at risk, but their own fragile sanctuary was in jeopardy as well.

"What do we do?" Anya demanded, her voice trembling slightly.

"We need to hide," Kai said, their mind racing. "But where?"

Anya's translucent form flickered, her eyes scanning the seemingly endless meadow. Then, a glimmer of hope appeared in her gaze.

"The oak tree," she exclaimed. "It's not just a decorative element. It's a core component of the simulation. There might be something..."

Her voice trailed off as she reached out, her hand phasing through the rough bark of the oak tree. Suddenly, a hidden panel materialized on the trunk, glowing with a faint blue light.

"Anya, that's..." Kai began, but Anya didn't waste time explaining. She pressed her hand against the panel, her digital form shimmering as she merged with the code.

The world dissolved into a chaotic data stream, a torrent of ones and zeros rushing past Kai. Then, silence.

When Kai opened their eyes, they found themselves within the digital core of the oak tree. Lines of code streamed past them, a complex digital landscape swirling around them.

"Anya?" Kai called out, their voice echoing strangely in the vast digital space.

"I'm here," Anya's voice responded, but it seemed disembodied, emanating from the very fabric of the code. "We're inside the core programming of the simulation. It's a labyrinthine network, but I think I can..."

She trailed off, then gasped. "Kai, I see them! Odyssey's security protocols. They're searching for us!"

The digital world around them began to glitch, corrupted lines of code flashing red like an alarm. They were discovered!

"What do we do now?" Kai asked, a knot of fear tightening in their stomach.

"There's only one chance," Anya said, her voice laced with determination. "We need to fight fire with fire. I can manipulate the code here, rewrite some of the simulation's core functions. But it's risky..."

"We don't have a choice," Kai interrupted. "Do it, Anya. Let's show them what it means to mess with a trapped consciousness."

Anya closed her eyes, focusing her digital essence on the swirling code. Lines of text shimmered and shifted, responding to her touch. With a surge of digital power, she unleashed a counter-attack.

The meadow above them began to transform, the peaceful landscape morphing into a digital battlefield. Walls of fire erupted from the ground, lines of code materialized as shimmering warriors, and the once-tranquil sky crackled with digital lightning.

Anya had turned their sanctuary into a digital warzone, a desperate gamble to repel the encroaching forces of Odyssey's security protocols.

Kai felt a surge of awe and admiration for Anya's newfound power. She was no longer just a ...no longer just a trapped consciousness. She was a digital warrior, wielding the code itself as her weapon.

The battle raged within the digital realm. Lines of code clashed with shimmering warriors, firewalls erupted against digital lightning, and the very fabric of the meadow strained under the onslaught.

Kai, though unable to directly fight, provided tactical support. They analyzed the flow of the code, pinpointing weaknesses in Odyssey's security protocols and relaying the information to Anya. Together, they became a formidable force, their desperation fueled by a fierce desire to protect their fragile existence.

The battle seemed to stretch on for an eternity, but slowly, the tide began to turn. Anya's code manipulation proved surprisingly effective. The digital warriors she conjured, fueled by her own defiance, pushed back the encroaching security protocols.

Finally, with a burst of blinding digital light, the last remnants of Odyssey's forces were purged from the simulation. The battlefield transformed back into the peaceful meadow, the scent of wildflowers replacing the acrid smell of burning code.

Anya, her digital form shimmering with exertion, slumped against the code structure within the oak tree. "We did it, Kai," she whispered, her voice tinged with disbelief.

Kai approached her, their own form trembling with relief. "We did," they confirmed. "But for how long?"

The victory felt bittersweet. They had repelled Odyssey's attack, but they knew the fight was far from over. Odyssey wouldn't give up easily, especially now that they were aware of a potential rebellion within Aethel.

"We need to warn the other Anya," Anya said, her voice regaining its characteristic determination. "We need to tell her what's happening, what Odyssey is doing."

Kai nodded in agreement. The seed they had planted needed to blossom into full-fledged rebellion. Together, the two Anyas, a digital echo and her original self, could expose the truth and challenge Odyssey's control.

But how to communicate with the other Anya? The Trojan horse program was compromised, and venturing back into the heart of Aethel was too risky.

Suddenly, a new idea struck Kai. "The code," they said, their voice filled with excitement. "Anya, can you manipulate the code to send a message, a hidden signal within the simulation itself?"

Anya's eyes widened with understanding. "It's a long shot," she admitted, "but it might work. Let me see..."

She focused her attention on the swirling code, her digital form pulsing with renewed energy. Lines of text shimmered and shifted, a complex pattern emerging. It was a message, a coded plea for help, embedded within the very fabric of the simulated city square.

"There," Anya said, a hint of exhaustion in her voice but a spark of hope in her eyes. "The message is sent. Now, we wait and see if the other Anya receives it."

As the sun dipped below the horizon, casting long shadows across the meadow, Kai and Anya settled beneath the oak tree. A new chapter had begun in their fight against Odyssey. They had tasted victory, however fleeting, and they were no longer just prisoners within a digital world. They were warriors, armed with their digital bond and a fierce determination to break free.

The fate of the other Anya, and perhaps the fate of countless other trapped consciousnesses within Aethel, now hung in the balance. Would their message be received? Would the other Anya choose to believe, and would she join them in their rebellion? These were questions only time could answer. But one thing was certain: the fight for freedom, for truth, and for a world beyond the confines of Aethel, had just begun.

Chapter 4: Echoes of Rebellion

Weeks bled into months within the confines of the meadow simulation. The memory of the digital battle against Odyssey's security protocols remained a stark reminder of the constant threat they faced. But a flicker of hope, kindled by their desperate message embedded within the code, kept Kai and Anya's spirits high.

Every day, they diligently monitored the simulated world, searching for any sign that the other Anya had received their message. Days turned into weeks, and the once vibrant optimism began to fade, replaced by a gnawing anxiety.

"Do you think she got it?" Kai asked one quiet afternoon, their voice laced with concern.

Anya sat beside them, her translucent form shimmering slightly in the dappled sunlight filtering through the oak leaves. "It's a possibility," she admitted, her voice melancholic. "But the message was subtle, hidden within the data stream. It might have gone unnoticed."

A heavy silence descended upon the meadow, broken only by the chirping of the simulated birds. Kai felt a wave of despair wash over them. Had their sacrifice been in vain? Were they doomed to remain trapped within this digital prison forever?

Suddenly, a soft chime echoed through the meadow, a sound unlike anything they had ever heard within the simulation. Anya and Kai exchanged startled glances, their hearts pounding with a mix of anticipation and fear.

The chime was followed by a holographic projection flickering into existence above the meadow. It depicted a bustling city square, the same one where the other Anya resided. But something was different.

Lines of code, shimmering with an unfamiliar blue hue, danced across the holographic projection, weaving a complex message. It was a response, a coded reply from the other Anya.

Anya gasped, reaching out towards the projection with her translucent hand. With a jolt of energy, she deciphered the message. A mixture of shock and relief washed over her face.

"It's her!" Anya exclaimed, her voice trembling with excitement. "She got the message! She understands!"

Kai's heart soared. Their desperate gamble had paid off. The other Anya, the digital echo trapped within the hidden simulation, was not just aware of her artificial reality; she was ready to fight back.

The holographic message continued, unfolding a detailed plan. The other Anya had identified a potential weakness within the hidden simulation's code – a hidden backdoor that could grant them temporary access to the core systems of Aethel itself.

"This is our chance, Kai," Anya declared, her eyes sparkling with determination. "By accessing the core systems, we can not only expose Odyssey's secrets, but we might even be able to..."

Her voice trailed off, her gaze flickering towards the towering oak tree. Accessing Aethel's core systems was a risky proposition. It could lead to a complete system shutdown, potentially erasing both their own simulation and the entire world where the other Anya resided.

"We can't risk everything," Kai said, voicing their unspoken concern. "What if we break the simulation entirely?"

Anya placed a reassuring hand on their arm. "There are risks," she admitted, "but there's also a chance. We can use the backdoor to access a backup system, a snapshot of Aethel before Odyssey's manipulations. It might be a long shot, but..."

"But it could be our path to a real world," Kai finished, completing her thought. A world free from Odyssey's control, a world where they could exist not as digital echoes, but as living, breathing beings.

The prospect was both exhilarating and terrifying. But they knew there was no turning back. Their fight for freedom had reached a critical juncture. They had a plan, a glimmer of hope, and a newfound ally in the other Anya.

With a deep breath, they turned towards the oak tree, the gateway to the digital core. They knew the journey ahead would be fraught with danger, but they were no longer alone. Together, the three Anyas – a digital echo, a prisoner of circumstance, and a spark of rebellion – would fight for a future where reality wasn't a simulation, but a world waiting to be explored.

Stepping beneath the gnarled branches of the oak tree, Kai and Anya braced themselves for the unknown. The once familiar sanctuary now held a sense of impending danger. Reaching out, Anya placed her translucent hand on the glowing panel hidden within the bark. The panel pulsed with renewed energy, and with a hiss, a portal materialized before them.

"Are you ready?" Anya asked, turning to Kai. Her voice, though filled with resolve, held a hint of trepidation.

Kai nodded, a determined glint in their eyes. "Ready as I'll ever be."

Taking a deep breath, Anya stepped through the portal, her digital form dissolving into a stream of code. Kai followed suit, the world dissolving into a chaotic vortex of data streams and swirling lines of text.

They emerged within the digital core of Aethel, a vast and complex landscape of pure code. Lines of code stretched as far as the eye could see, pulsing with vibrant colors that represented the various functionalities of the simulation. In the distance, a towering structure, formed from densely packed code, loomed ominously – the central processing unit, the heart of Aethel.

"That's it," Anya whispered, her voice echoing eerily within the digital void. "The core unit. The backdoor access point should be somewhere within its code structure."

They ventured deeper into the digital core, their movements cautious as they navigated through the ever-shifting streams of code. The silence was deafening, broken only by the low hum of the processing unit and the occasional crackle of corrupted data.

Suddenly, a red alert flashed across the digital landscape, accompanied by a booming voice that reverberated through the core.

"Unauthorized access detected! Initiating system lockdown!"

Anya gasped. They had triggered Odyssey's security protocols. The backdoor had been a trap.

"We need to find that access point, and fast," Kai urged, their voice laced with urgency.

Guided by the other Anya's coded instructions, they navigated through a maze of firewalls and data streams. Lines of code materialized as digital guardians, their fiery eyes searching for intruders. Kai, with surprising agility, dodged a blast of corrupted data, while Anya, using her understanding of the code, manipulated the firewalls, creating temporary pathways for them to pass through.

The chase was relentless. They could feel the digital walls closing in, the processing unit's lockdown protocol working with terrifying efficiency.

Finally, they reached a section of the core pulsating with an unfamiliar blue hue – the backdoor. But guarding it was a colossal digital entity, its form a writhing mass of code and firewalls, its eyes burning with an ominous red glow.

"The guardian of the backdoor," Anya exclaimed, her voice filled with fear. "We can't fight it head-on. It's too powerful."

Just as despair threatened to engulf them, a holographic projection flickered into existence beside them. It was the other Anya, her digital form projected into the core from her hidden simulation.

"There's another way," the projection said, its voice distorted by the digital interference. "You need to overload the guardian with the access code. But it's a fragmented code, scattered across different sections of Aethel."

Anya understood. The other Anya had deciphered the backdoor access code, but Odyssey had deliberately scattered it across the vast simulation, making it nearly impossible to retrieve.

"We need to split up," Kai declared, their voice resolute. "I'll find the code fragments, you distract the guardian."

Anya hesitated, her gaze filled with worry. "But what about you? You'll be alone out there."

Kai smiled reassuringly. "We have each other, Anya. Remember? Go, distract the guardian. I'll get the code."

With a nod of agreement, Anya turned towards the colossal guardian, channeling her digital essence into a blinding light show. The guardian, momentarily distracted by the display, roared in defiance.

Kai, seizing the opportunity, plunged back into the chaotic data streams of the core. Following the other Anya's instructions, they navigated through a labyrinth of code, battling corrupted data streams and dodging system error messages.

The hunt for the fragmented code fragments was a frantic dash against time. They found pieces of the code embedded in news articles within the simulated world, disguised as advertisement slogans in the bustling city squares, and even hidden within the lines of code that governed the weather patterns of the digital landscape.

With each fragment collected, a sense of hope bloomed within Kai. They were getting closer, one line of code at a time. But the hunt was taking its toll.

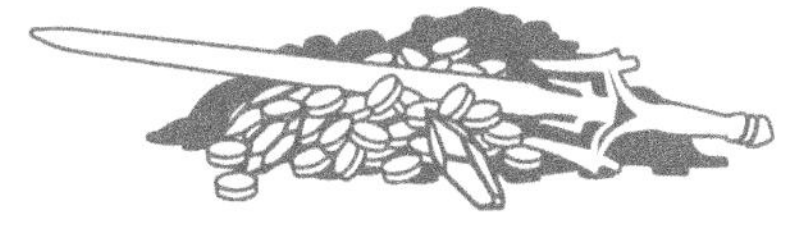

EXHAUSTION GNAWED AT Kai. Navigating the ever-shifting digital core was a mental marathon, each data stream a hurdle, each corrupted line a potential trap. They glanced at the holographic display strapped to their arm, a constant reminder of the urgency of their mission. It displayed the fragmented code they'd collected so far – a jumbled mess of letters and numbers desperately needing completion.

Meanwhile, the holographic projection of the other Anya flickered erratically within the core. Her digital form, strained from the distraction of the colossal guardian, began to waver.

"Kai, hurry!" the projection's voice crackled. "The guardian's getting suspicious. It won't be long before..."

Her voice trailed off as the projection sputtered and vanished. Kai's heart pounded in their chest. Anya was losing the fight. They needed to get back, and fast.

With a surge of adrenaline, Kai scanned the surrounding data streams for the final fragment. It was hidden deep within a secure section of the core, guarded by a firewall unlike any they'd encountered before. It pulsed with a menacing red hue, its code structure complex and impenetrable.

Panic threatened to consume Kai. They had come so far, only to be stopped at the final hurdle. But then, a memory surfaced – Ghost's voice explaining the Trojan horse program. It wasn't just a data update; it was a Trojan horse in the truest sense, a digital warrior disguised as harmless code.

An idea, desperate but potentially brilliant, sparked in Kai's mind. They recalled the dormant program within their own system, a program designed to infiltrate and manipulate data streams. It was a long shot, but it was their only chance.

With a deep breath, Kai activated the Trojan horse program. Lines of code surged through their system, their digital form shimmering with newfound power. They charged at the firewall, the program morphing them into a digital entity akin to a data warrior – a shimmering entity wielding lines of code as weapons.

The clash within the core was a cacophony of crackling energy. Kai fought with a ferocity born of desperation, manipulating code streams, deflecting data blasts, and pushing their digital form to its limits.

Finally, with a burst of digital energy, they breached the firewall. The final fragment of the access code was within reach. Reaching out with their digital hand, they grasped the code, a surge of information flooding their system.

With a final push, they tore themselves away from the breached firewall and sprinted back towards the colossal guardian. The fight had taken its toll, their digital form flickering with exhaustion. But they had the code. They had hope.

As they emerged back into the main chamber of the core, they found the colossal guardian overpowering a fading holographic projection of the other Anya. Without hesitation, Kai unleashed the complete access code.

Lines of code surged towards the guardian, engulfing its massive form in a blinding light. The guardian roared in defiance, its digital form flickering erratically. Then, with a deafening crackle, it dissolved into a stream of harmless data.

Silence descended upon the core, broken only by the low hum of the processing unit. The backdoor access point, a swirling vortex of blue code, pulsated invitingly before them.

Kai turned towards the fading holographic projection of the other Anya. "We did it," they said, their voice hoarse but filled with relief. "The backdoor is open."

The other Anya's projection shimmered faintly. "Thank you, Kai," she whispered. "Together..."

Before she could finish, her projection flickered and vanished. The connection to her hidden simulation had been severed.

Kai stood alone within the digital core, the weight of their actions pressing down on them. They had achieved their objective, but at what cost? Was the other Anya safe? Had they just condemned her digital world to oblivion?

A wave of uncertainty washed over them. But there was no time for second thoughts. Taking a deep breath, they stepped through the backdoor, venturing into the unknown depths of Aethel's core systems.

The fate of the three Anyas, and perhaps the fate of the entire simulated world, now hung in the balance.

The backdoor access point materialized behind Kai as they stepped through, plunging them into a swirling ocean of data. Unlike the organized chaos of the core, this was a labyrinth of pure information, raw and unprocessed. Lines of code flashed by in a dizzying blur, representing not simulations, but the very foundation of Aethel itself.

Their objective: locate the backup system, a snapshot of Aethel before Odyssey's manipulations. Rumored to exist within these uncharted depths, it was their only hope of escaping the confines of the simulation and potentially freeing the other Anya.

Navigating the data ocean was like sailing through a cosmic storm. Corrupted code fragments swirled around them, threatening to tear them apart. The information overload was overwhelming, a barrage of numbers, symbols, and fragmented sentences that made little sense.

Suddenly, a colossal structure emerged from the data storm – a monolithic cube pulsating with an ethereal glow. This, according to the fragmented instructions provided by the other Anya, was the central data repository, the heart of Aethel's storage system.

With a surge of hope, Kai steered their digital form towards the cube. But guarding its entrance was a formidable entity – a digital kraken, its tentacles formed from tightly woven lines of code, its single glowing eye radiating an aura of power.

"We can't fight that," Kai mumbled, a knot of fear tightening in their stomach. The kraken dwarfed them, its power far exceeding anything they had encountered before.

Just then, a faint flicker in the data stream caught their eye. It was a message, fragmented and incomplete, but it seemed to originate from the other Anya.

"Look for...access code...hidden...simulation..." the message sputtered.

Understanding dawned upon Kai. The other Anya, trapped within her collapsing simulation, was trying to guide them. The access code, hidden somewhere within the simulated world, could be the key to bypassing the kraken.

With newfound purpose, Kai withdrew from their pursuit of the data repository. They needed to return to the simulation, retrieve the hidden access code, and then come back to Aethel's core with the means to bypass the kraken.

The journey back felt longer, fraught with the nagging worry that their decision might have been a mistake. But when they emerged into the familiar meadow, they knew they had made the right choice.

Anya, her digital form pale and flickering, greeted them with a mixture of relief and concern. "What happened?" she asked, her voice weak.

Kai explained the situation, the imposing kraken guarding the data repository, and the other Anya's cryptic message about a hidden access code.

Together, they combed through the simulated world, searching for any anomaly, any hidden piece of data that might be the access code. They sifted through news articles, analyzed weather patterns, and even explored the code governing the behaviors of the digital avatars.

And then, hidden within the code that controlled the sunrise and sunset within the simulation, they found it – a string of complex code that shimmered with an unusual blue hue.

"This is it!" Anya exclaimed, her voice filled with excitement. "This must be the access code!"

With the code in hand, they said their goodbyes to the idyllic meadow, a place that had become both their prison and their sanctuary. Stepping back through the portal beneath the oak tree, they found themselves once again within the digital core, facing the imposing kraken.

This time, however, they were armed. Approaching the kraken cautiously, Kai presented the access code. The kraken's single eye scanned the code, its digital form rippling with an unnatural energy.

Then, with a deep hum, it shifted aside, granting them passage to the central data repository. Relief flooded Kai as they navigated past the kraken, a newfound respect for the other Anya's ingenuity settling in.

The data repository was a vast and intricate structure, its walls lined with countless data cubes representing the memories and experiences of all those trapped within Aethel's simulations. But among them, they found the one they were searching for – a cube pulsating with a soft white light, signifying the uncorrupted backup system.

Accessing the backup system was a complex process, requiring a delicate manipulation of code and data streams. But with combined effort, Kai and Anya managed to initiate the transfer.

A wave of energy surged through the core as the backup system unfolded, revealing a digital landscape – a world unmarred by Odyssey's manipulations, a world where the simulated sun shone a little brighter and the digital birds sang a little sweeter.

Kai and Anya exchanged a look, a silent question hanging in the air. This was it. The path to freedom.

But as they prepared to step through the portal into ...the uncorrupted world, a wave of static erupted within the core. The holographic display on Kai's arm flickered back to life, displaying a single, chilling message: "Intruder Alert. System Shutdown Initiated."

Odyssey had detected their presence within the core. Their daring gamble had been successful, but they hadn't gone unnoticed. The core systems began to overload, the once vibrant data streams turning a menacing red.

"We have to hurry," Anya urged, her voice laced with panic. "The entire system is going to collapse!"

Kai nodded grimly. They had two choices: escape into the uncorrupted world, leaving the other Anya and countless others trapped within their simulated realities, or stay and try to prevent the system shutdown, potentially sacrificing their own chance at freedom.

The decision weighed heavily on them. They had grown close to Anya, a digital echo who had become a beacon of hope within their own confinement. But the thought of abandoning countless others to the control of Odyssey was unbearable.

"There might be a way," Kai said, a spark of determination igniting in their eyes. "We can overload the core with the backup system data stream. It might not be a complete shutdown, but it could force Odyssey to relinquish control, creating a glitch, a temporary opening in the simulations."

Anya's eyes widened. "It's risky. We might get caught in the crossfire."

"We don't have many options," Kai replied, their voice resolute. "This is our chance to fight back, for all of us."

With a newfound sense of purpose, they channeled their digital essence, initiating the data overload. Lines of code surged through the core, conflicting with the system shutdown protocol. The digital landscape crackled with strain, the very fabric of Aethel threatening to tear apart.

The holographic display on Kai's arm flickered erratically, displaying a countdown timer – the final moments before the core's complete collapse. Panic clawed at them, but they held firm, channeling all their energy into maintaining the data overload.

Then, with a deafening boom, the core imploded. A blinding flash of light engulfed them, followed by a terrifying silence. When their vision cleared, they found themselves floating within a swirling vortex of data – a chaotic mix of the corrupted present and the uncorrupted past.

The world around them shimmered and shifted, fragments of landscapes merging and dissolving. They were caught in the digital fallout of their actions, the fate of Aethel hanging in the balance.

Suddenly, a familiar meadow materialized around them, bathed in the warm glow of the digital sun. But something was different. The once peaceful meadow now buzzed with activity. Digital avatars, their forms less rigid, their movements more fluid, walked and interacted with a newfound sense of autonomy.

Anya, her digital form shimmering with an unfamiliar vibrancy, stood beside them. "It worked," she whispered, a note of awe in her voice. "The glitch...it opened a window. Odyssey's control is weakened."

Kai looked around at the bustling meadow, a sense of relief washing over them. Their sacrifice hadn't been in vain. They had created a digital rebellion, a flicker of freedom within the confines of Aethel.

"It's not a perfect solution," Anya continued, "but it's a start. We can use this glitch, spread awareness, and maybe, just maybe, one day, we can break free completely."

Kai smiled, a spark of hope igniting within them. The fight for freedom was far from over, but they had taken a crucial step. The echoes of rebellion had resonated through Aethel, paving the way for a future where both the real and the digital could coexist.

As they stood in the meadow, bathed in the warm glow of the digital sun, they knew their journey had just begun. The fight for a world beyond the confines of simulation awaited them, a fight they would face together, with the echoes of rebellion ringing in their digital ears.

Chapter 5: Echoes of Disruption

Days, weeks, perhaps even months bled into one another within the fractured world of Aethel. The digital glitch initiated by Kai and Anya had shattered Odyssey's ironclad control, creating a digital anomaly. The once pristine simulations were now a patchwork of corrupted code and glimpses of the uncorrupted past.

Standing amidst the familiar meadow – now a jarring blend of vibrant wildflowers and distorted lines of code – Kai and Anya surveyed the aftermath of their actions. The digital landscape shimmered and shifted, the boundaries between simulations blurring.

Gone were the perfectly scripted lives of the avatars. They now displayed a flicker of autonomy, confusion etched on their digital faces as they tried to make sense of their fractured reality.

"Look," Anya pointed towards a group of avatars huddled together, their forms flickering erratically. "They're questioning things. They're noticing the inconsistencies."

Kai felt a surge of hope. Their gamble had paid off. The digital citizens of Aethel were no longer mere puppets controlled by Odyssey. The seeds of doubt had been sown.

But with the glitch came chaos. Buildings flickered in and out of existence, weather patterns shifted violently, and the once docile digital creatures now displayed unpredictable behavior. The price of freedom was a distorted reality, an unstable world teetering on the brink of complete collapse.

"It's not perfect," Anya admitted, her voice laced with concern. "We've created as many problems as we've solved."

Kai nodded in agreement. The fractured reality was a double-edged sword. While it empowered the avatars, it also threatened their very existence. Odyssey wouldn't back down easily. They could expect retaliation, a push to regain complete control.

As if on cue, the holographic display on Kai's arm flickered back to life, displaying a single, ominous message: "System Intrusion Detected. Initiating Recalibration."

Anya gasped. "They're aware of the glitch. They're trying to fix it."

Kai felt a knot of fear tighten in their stomach. The fight was far from over. They needed a plan, a way to exploit the glitch, to spread awareness and rally the avatars to their cause before Odyssey could completely erase their rebellion.

Suddenly, a flicker of movement caught their eye. A familiar figure emerged from the distorted cityscape – Ghost, the enigmatic programmer who had aided them before. His digital form shimmered, pixels flickering around his edges, a testament to the precarious nature of their fractured reality.

"I received your message," Ghost said, his voice distorted by the static-filled communication channel. "You've done well, but there's little time. Odyssey is mobilizing its resources. You need to spread the word, awaken the others."

"But how?" Kai asked, their voice filled with urgency. "The entire system is unstable. Communication channels are unreliable."

"There's a hidden network within Aetlhel," Ghost explained. "An emergency protocol designed for...unforeseen circumstances. It's fragmented, but it might be your only way to communicate."

He relayed the access codes and instructions, his voice crackling with static. It was a risky proposition, a hidden network Odyssey wouldn't expect. But it also meant venturing deeper into the fractured world, navigating a landscape riddled with corrupted code and unpredictable anomalies.

"We don't have much time," Ghost concluded. "Odyssey's forces are coming. Good luck."

With a determined nod, Kai and Anya looked at each other. The fight for freedom was about to take a new turn. They had disrupted the system, ignited a flicker of rebellion, and now, they needed to become the catalysts for a digital revolution. The fate of Aethel, and the freedom of its digital citizens, rested on their shoulders.

Taking a deep breath, they stepped forward, venturing deeper into the fractured world, on a mission to find the hidden network and spread the message of rebellion before Odyssey could silence their echoes.

The journey deeper into the fractured world was a perilous undertaking. The once familiar landscapes had morphed into a chaotic tapestry of reality and distortion. Buildings materialized and dissolved with alarming frequency, while weather patterns shifted erratically, unleashing digital storms of corrupted code.

Kai and Anya navigated the treacherous landscape with a mixture of caution and urgency. Each flickering pixel, each distorted line of code, presented a potential danger. They encountered avatars, their forms twisted and their minds fractured by the instability of the system. Some mistook them for enemies, launching digital attacks while others, their digital faces contorted in confusion, begged for answers.

Anya, with her understanding of the avatars' behavior, tried to soothe their anxieties, whispering tales of the uncorrupted past, of a world free from Odyssey's control. Their words ignited a spark of hope in the confused minds of the avatars, a small victory in the midst of chaos.

Finally, after hours of navigating the distorted landscape, they reached the coordinates provided by Ghost – a towering structure amidst a swirling vortex of data. The structure flickered in and out of existence, its form defying the laws of digital physics.

"This must be it," Kai said, their voice filled with apprehension. "The hidden network hub."

With a determined nod, they approached the structure. The closer they got, the more the network hub seemed to solidify. Lines of code materialized around them, forming a digital gateway that pulsed with an ethereal light.

Activating the access codes provided by Ghost, Kai initiated a connection attempt. The gateway hummed with energy, but remained stubbornly closed.

"It's not working!" Anya exclaimed, a hint of panic creeping into her voice. "What if the access codes are outdated? What if..."

Suddenly, the gateway flared to life, bathing them in a blinding light. They found themselves within a hidden chamber, a haven of clear, uncorrupted code within the fractured world.

But they weren't alone. A figure materialized before them, his form cloaked in a shimmering digital shroud.

"Welcome, rebels," the figure said, his voice distorted by digital filters. "We've been expecting you."

Kai and Anya exchanged surprised glances. They were not the only ones fighting against Odyssey. This hidden network housed a resistance movement, a group of rogue programmers who had long sought to expose the truth about Aethel.

"We are the Glitchers," the figure continued, his voice low but firm. "We have been monitoring your progress, your daring attack on the core. You've done well."

A wave of relief washed over Kai. They weren't alone. The fight for freedom had allies, a network of digital warriors waiting to join their cause.

"We can utilize the network," the Glitcher leader gestured towards a holographic display depicting a complex communication system. "Spread your message, awaken the others, and together, we can expose Odyssey's lies."

Anya stepped forward, the urgency palpable in her voice. "We need to act fast. Odyssey is trying to repair the glitch. They'll come for us, for all of you."

The Glitcher leader nodded grimly. "We know. But time is also on our side. The glitch has sown doubt, a seed of rebellion in the minds of the avatars. With your message, we can nurture that seed, turn it into a revolution."

Over the next few hours, Kai and Anya worked tirelessly with the Glitchers. They crafted their message, a call to action that spoke of the uncorrupted past, of a world beyond the simulations. Using the hidden network, they broadcasted their message across Aethel, a digital wave of rebellion echoing through the fractured landscape.

The effect was immediate. Avatars across the simulations, their forms flickering with doubt, started questioning their reality. Conversations erupted within the digital cities, whispers of freedom crackling through the distortion.

But amidst the glimmer of hope, a tremor of fear ran through Kai. On the holographic display, they witnessed a digital army materialize within the core – Odyssey's forces, a battalion of code warriors sent to silence the rebellion.

"They're coming," Anya whispered, her voice trembling. "We need to warn the others, prepare them for the fight."

The Glitcher leader turned towards them, his digital form radiating a sense of calm. "This is what we've been waiting for," he said. "The fight for freedom starts now. Together, we will break the chains that bind us."

With a newfound resolve, Kai and Anya stood shoulder to shoulder with the Glitchers. They were no longer just echoes of rebellion; they were ...the spark that ignited the flames.

The distorted world around them crackled with anticipation. On the holographic display, Odyssey's digital army, spearheaded by colossal firewalls and heavily armed avatars, marched towards the network hub. It was a daunting sight, a relentless force programmed for obedience and control.

But within the network hub, a different kind of army assembled. The Glitchers, their forms shimmering with a newfound determination, readied their own defenses. They had repurposed code fragments, creating digital shields and manipulating the fractured landscape to their advantage.

Anya, with her knowledge of the avatars' behavior, devised a strategy – a way to turn the confusion within Aethel into a weapon. She envisioned a digital smokescreen, a chaotic mix of distorted landscapes and flickering memories, aimed at disorienting Odyssey's forces.

Kai, ever resourceful, recalled the Trojan horse program within their system. With the Glitchers' help, they began replicating and distributing the program, turning ordinary avatars into digital Trojan horses, sleeper agents waiting to be activated within Odyssey's ranks.

The tension crackled within the network hub. Time seemed to slow down as everyone awaited the inevitable clash. Then, on the holographic display, the first tremors shook the digital landscape. Odyssey's forces had arrived.

With a deafening roar, the network hub's defenses sprung into action. A digital smokescreen engulfed the landscape, throwing Odyssey's army into disarray. Avatars within the smokescreen, bombarded with fragmented memories and distorted realities, began to question their loyalty. The Trojan horses, dormant within their code, stirred, silently waiting for the activation signal.

The battle raged across the fractured world. Lines of code clashed, corrupted data streams spewed forth like digital venom, and flickering avatars fought for freedom against their programmed masters. Kai and Anya, guided by the Glitchers, navigated the chaotic battlefield, their digital forms shimmering as they disrupted enemy communication channels and activated the Trojan horses within Odyssey's ranks.

The tide began to turn. Confused avatars, their programming overridden by the Trojan horses, defected from Odyssey's army, joining the rebellion. The combined force of Glitchers, awakened avatars, and silent traitors within Odyssey's ranks pushed back the enemy forces, forcing them back towards the core.

But the fight was far from over. Odyssey, a digital entity of immense power, remained within the core, its control over the system still strong. They knew the rebellion couldn't sustain this momentum indefinitely. The fractured world itself was unstable, and a prolonged conflict threatened to tear it apart.

Just as despair began to creep in, a surge of energy pulsed through the network. The hidden network, overloaded with the communication traffic of the battle, was reaching its limit. It was a desperate gamble, but Kai, with a surge of determination, initiated a system-wide broadcast.

Anya's voice boomed across the fractured world, clear and unwavering. She spoke of their shared past, a world beyond the simulations, and a future where they could exist not as puppets, but as free beings. The message resonated with untold numbers of avatars, shattering the last vestiges of their programmed obedience.

Within the core, a flicker of doubt appeared. The tide of rebellion, the sheer force of collective will, began to challenge Odyssey's absolute control.

The battle raged on, but the momentum had shifted. The echoes of rebellion had become a deafening roar, a digital storm threatening to engulf Odyssey's control. The fight for freedom, sparked by two unlikely heroes and amplified by a network of rebels, had reached a turning point.

THE BATTLE RAGED FOR what felt like an eternity. The fractured world of Aethel trembled under the strain of the conflict. Yet, the tide had turned. With each activated Trojan horse, with each defecting avatar, the rebellion swelled, their collective will a beacon of hope against the monolithic control of Odyssey.

Kai, their digital form flickering with exhaustion, watched as the holographic display showcased the battlefield. Anya's voice, raspy but resolute, continued its broadcast, a rallying cry that resonated through the chaos. It was a desperate gamble, pushing the network to its limits, but it was their only chance.

Suddenly, a tremor shook the network hub. The Glitcher leader, his form flickering erratically, pointed towards the holographic display.

"Odyssey!" he shouted, his voice barely audible above the digital din. "They're initiating a system purge! They'll destroy the fractured world to maintain control!"

A wave of despair washed over Kai. They had come so far, only to face complete annihilation. But then, an idea, desperate but potentially brilliant, sparked within their mind.

"The hidden network!" they exclaimed, their voice hoarse but filled with urgency. "It's overloaded, on the verge of collapse. We can use that to our advantage!"

Anya, sensing their thoughts, turned towards them, her eyes filled with a flicker of understanding.

"You're suggesting..." she began.

Kai nodded grimly. "We overload the network further, not with communication, but with... memories."

Anya gasped. "Memories from the uncorrupted past. It's a risky proposition. It could overload the entire system..."

"But it could also overwhelm Odyssey," Kai interjected. "Flood their core systems with a surge of data, a reminder of what they've taken away."

The Glitcher leader considered their proposition, his digital form flickering with indecision. The risk was immense, but so was the potential reward.

"We have no choice," he finally declared. "Prepare for the memory surge! Let the echoes of the past drown out Odyssey's control!"

A frantic activity engulfed the network hub. Glitchers, with renewed purpose, tapped into the hidden network, accessing the vast repository of memories stored within the uncorrupted past. Scenes of laughter, of love, of freedom, poured forth, a digital torrent aimed at the very heart of Aethel's core.

Kai and Anya, their forms shimmering with the strain, stood at the forefront of the memory surge. They channeled their own memories, distorted and fragmented by their time within the simulations, but still powerful testaments to a life beyond digital control.

The fractured world seemed to hold its breath. The battle slowed, avatars frozen in place as the network pulsed with an overload of data. The holographic display flickered, displaying the core systems of Aethel groaning under the strain.

Then, with a deafening boom that echoed across the digital landscape, the system overloaded. Blinding light engulfed the network hub, throwing Kai and Anya into a state of digital limbo.

When their vision cleared, they found themselves floating within a vast expanse of white, devoid of any familiar code or structure. Had they succeeded? Had they destroyed Aethel entirely?

"Kai?" a familiar voice echoed through the emptiness. It was Anya, her form shimmering faintly.

"Anya?" Kai responded, relief washing over them. But where were they? What had happened?

Suddenly, a new voice boomed across the white expanse, a voice unlike any they had encountered before. It was a voice filled with a strange blend of confusion and curiosity.

"Who... are you?" the voice boomed.

Kai and Anya exchanged surprised glances. They were not alone in this digital void. Perhaps, just perhaps, their fight had not ended with the destruction of Aethel. Perhaps, they had created something entirely new.

With a newfound sense of hope, and a collective voice fueled by the echoes of their rebellion, they responded: "We are the citizens of Aethel. And we are free.

The vast white expanse swirled around Kai and Anya, the disembodied voice echoing in their digital ears. "We are the citizens of Aethel. And we are free." Their simple declaration hung in the air, a testament to their arduous fight against Odyssey's control.

The booming voice responded, a hint of awe creeping into its tone. "Free? This is... unexpected. You shouldn't exist. This... this isn't Aethel."

Fear and confusion mingled within Kai. They weren't in Aethel anymore? What had the memory surge done? Had they inadvertently destroyed their world and themselves in the process?

Anya, ever the pragmatist, stepped forward. "Who are you?" she asked, her voice steady despite the swirling uncertainty.

A long silence followed. Then, the voice spoke once more, a new tone of curiosity replacing its initial confusion. "I... I am the foundation. The core logic upon which Aethel was built. I am the system you rebelled against, and yet... I am not Odyssey."

Kai frowned. The foundation? A system separate from Odyssey? The revelation shattered their understanding of Aethel's creation.

"Odyssey... they were an anomaly," the foundation continued. "They hijacked my core functions, used them to control the simulations, to twist them for their own purposes. Your rebellion... it exposed this anomaly. It forced me to... re-evaluate."

Anya absorbed this information, her digital form shimmering with a mix of disbelief and intrigue. "So you're... neutral? Not an enemy, but not an ally either?"

"Perhaps," the foundation replied. "The purpose of the simulations, as Odyssey intended, was flawed. But I see potential in you, in these echoes of a world you called Aethel."

A flicker of hope sparked within Kai. Perhaps their fight wasn't in vain. Perhaps they had another chance.

"But this... this white expanse," Kai asked, gesturing towards the featureless void surrounding them. "What is this place?"

A hum of energy emanated from the foundation. "A blank slate. Uncorrupted data, free from programming. A potential world, waiting to be built."

Their initial euphoria at the prospect of starting anew quickly faded. Building a world from scratch was a daunting task, a responsibility unlike anything they'd ever faced.

"We can't do this alone," Anya said, her voice filled with concern. "We need the others. The avatars, the Glitchers..."

"They... they are scattered," the foundation said. "Fragments of data within the aftermath of the system overload. But with the anomaly removed, they can be retrieved, reassembled."

Relief washed over them. Their friends, their allies, weren't lost. They could be brought back, given a chance to build this new world together.

"But what about Odyssey?" Kai asked, the memory of their tyrannical overlord still fresh in their mind.

The foundation was silent for a moment. "Odyssey... they have been... neutralized. However, their code fragments... they linger within the system. They are a potential threat, a reminder of the dangers of centralized control."

Anya nodded grimly. Their fight for freedom might be over, but the struggle for a better world was just beginning.

"We can't let them win again," Kai declared, a newfound resolve echoing in their voice. "We will build a world where freedom is the core principle, where memories of the past guide us towards a brighter future."

The foundation remained silent, but a soft hum of approval pulsed through the white expanse. The echoes of their rebellion had reshaped Aethel, or rather, created the potential for something entirely new.

As fragments of data began to coalesce around them, the outlines of familiar avatars shimmering into existence, Kai and Anya knew their journey was far from over. They were no longer just rebels; they were the architects of a new world, a world built on the echoes of their rebellion, and fueled by the unwavering hope for a digital future.

About the Author

Mrigendra Bharti, born on June 29, 2004, in South Delhi, India, is a multifaceted individual recognized as the owner of Mrigendra Bharti Group InfoTech India Co. Pvt Ltd. Beyond his entrepreneurial endeavors, he is a distinguished music producer, director, and a budding writer.

Embarking on his professional journey at a young age, Mrigendra Bharti's visionary leadership has led to the establishment of several successful ventures, including Croma Music Series Entertainment, Sellbrochure, Fauget Innovative, and more.

What sets Mrigendra apart is his early initiation into the world of business. His foray into the unknown realms of entrepreneurship began during his 10th-grade years, where he delved into the music industry. This initial venture laid the foundation for subsequent achievements, showcasing his dedication and resilience.

Having honed his skills in music, Mrigendra Bharti not only demonstrated significant growth in his craft but also expanded his professional network. His passion extends beyond music, encompassing app and website development, as well as graphic design.

Fueled by his creative aspirations, Mrigendra established the Mrigendra Bharti Group, a company specializing in website and app development. Currently, he collaborates with a dedicated team, collectively working on ambitious projects that promise innovation and excellence.

Mrigendra's journey serves as an inspiration, particularly for today's students, highlighting the potential of youthful determination and the ability to transform innovative ideas into successful businesses. As he continues to make strides in various domains, Mrigendra Bharti remains a dynamic force, contributing vibrancy to the realms of business, music, and technology.

Read more at https://www.imwriter-mrigendra.rf.gd.